If My Dog Could Drive

Bernice Lum

Bloomsbury Children's Books

If my dog could drive ...

For Mom and Pops

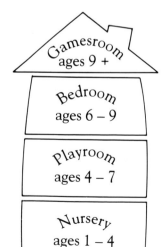

Gamesroom
ages 9 +

Bedroom
ages 6 – 9

Playroom
ages 4 – 7

Nursery
ages 1 – 4

Our Bloomsbury Book House
has a special room for each
age group -
this one is from the Nursery.

First published in Great Britain in 1995.
Text and illustration copyright (c) 1995 Bernice Lum
The moral right of the author has been assured
Bloomsbury Publishing PLC, 2 Soho Square, London W1V 5DF
A CIP catalogue record for this book is available from The British Library
Manufactured in China

ISBN 0747520704

he would drive the stars in a stretch limousine.

He could putter about on a motorcycle ...

or drive cross country in an old jeep.

I know he would love to drive a big red fire engine!

He could drive a black cab in London ...

or a yellow cab in New York.

He could even drive a huge lorry ...

with his favourite biscuits inside.

He could take it slow on a tractor ...

or *speed* around in a racing car.

It would be fun to drive his friends on a train.

Choo choo!

In the end though ...

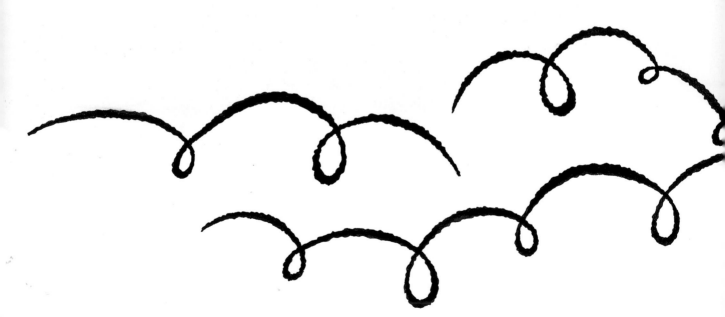

I think Stanley would prefer me to drive!